VALENTINE DARE

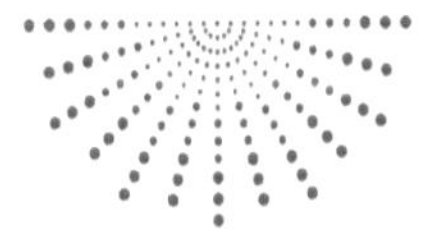

SARWAH CREED

Hi Lovey Reader,

I'm so excited that you've decided to pick up my new release, and read it.

I really hope you are going to enjoy it.

If you do, and you would love to read more of my books, then do not hesitate to contact me on social media. I'm even on Tiktok!

Have a great year, and happy reading.

Sarwah

ABOUT SARWAH CREED

Sarwah Creed is the author of The FlirtChat series. When she's not writing, then she's running, reading and listening to music. She lives with her three children in Madrid.

Learn more about Sarwah by connecting with her on social media:

Newsletter ---- http://eepurl.com/g0cLoH

The three jocks wanted me to tutor them, but I had no intention of doing it for free!

I was supposed to be happy and move on to a new era. One every high-schooler craves. Yet, the bullying hasn't stopped, and my eating habits are way out of control. I've gotten to a stage where I don't care about anything anymore.

Until Principal Williams called me into his office and asked me to tutor not one jock, but all three of them. As each day went by, my hot, annoying students took less of an interest in studying every day, and more of an interest in me.

I dared them!

I wanted to make the one girl in high school who made my life a misery know what it was like to be on the receiving end.

And it worked!

Author's Note:

Valentine Dare is a stand-alone reverse harem with a mixture of romance, humor, and even suspense. There are multiple partner

scenes, so make sure that not only is your Kindle ready, but you have a towel nearby too as you read this hot stand-alone HEA.

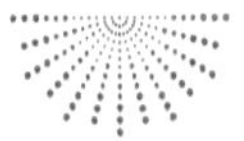

eese

"*R*eese Smith please go to Principal Williams' office immediately!"

It was announced on the loudspeaker of Chaparral Elementary School and I cringed at hearing my name once again being called out loud. I wanted to hide, make everyone forget I was here. That way I would have a peaceful life. I wouldn't have body-sized knickers stretched over six lockers, with a note saying Reese Smith left these at my house.

Or videos of me running, something I try to avoid like the plague, but with physical ed there were only so many times I could fake not being part of the class. The rest of the time, I was filmed, even though no one should have their phone. Someone always managed to go to such lengths to humiliate me on social media.

Either way, I didn't feel like going to Principal Williams' office after the morning I had, when everyone started snorting like a pig as I walked into class. Jade Baxter, my ex-best friend and now nemesis, decided to post a video of me running in class with my head replaced as a pig sweating, and my body stretched so I looked a lot bigger than I was, and she wanted everyone to see it. Posting it on Instagram, wasn't enough. Nor Snapchat. She made sure it was on the projector playing as I walked into class. Mr. Humphrey walked in and turned it off, but it was too late because her plan had worked. Everyone had seen it. Including me.

I had a love-hate relationship with Principal Williams because he was my Godfather. A secret we both kept. If it'd gotten out then they would have something else to tease and torture me about, and I didn't need it. Neither did he, he hated the attention.

"Go in." Beth, his secretary, shifted her head to the side as I walked to his office. She knew what I was doing here, and she had the same sympathetic look on her face every time I turned up.

We'd gone from her having small talk, asking about my day and all, to telling me to go in as she was doing today. I didn't know whether to be happy that we'd skipped the first step, and gone to the just go in his office, or not.

With my head slouched, as if all the world's problems were sitting on top of it, my sweaty palm reached for the door handle, but before I could even open the door, the choice was taken out of my hand.

"We were about to send a search party for you." Principal Williams smiled as my eyes met his face. I had dragged my feet headed this way, but I didn't think I was walking slowly, especially because every part of me was sweating, and it was obvious as I felt a drop of sweat leave my forehead. I used my sweaty palm to rub my head as he moved aside and I entered his office.

I'd only been to the principal's office here at Chaparral Elementary, so I couldn't compare it to any other Principal's office, but I had a feeling if I did then all their offices would be the same. Awards on the wall, chestnut desk, and trophies from way back when sat on the shelves.

I was about to say something when I saw we weren't alone. I would have asked him if he was coming over this weekend or anything to break the ice, and get rid of the butterflies in my stomach.

Howard Pete, the Quarterback and the better half of the one girl in high school who loved to hate me, was sitting and clearly irritated. His blue eyes darted my way and then focused on the front, as if he was back in a trance. He ignored me in school, so I shouldn't expect any difference in the Principal's office.

His best friend, Alan Smith, was here, too. It was as if they were pretending to know each other, as his hand traced over his short afro, and didn't look my way. And Jeff James, the captain of the baseball team. His dark eyes shifted my way, and then back to the floor. He wasn't much different from Jade. If he had a chance, he would be posting things on social media, too. But he didn't, he spent his time teasing and taunting me in the cafeteria. So I made sure I spent most of my time avoiding him like the plague and not entering whenever he was there.

"Well, I called you all here. Reese please sit down."

I nodded, and saw the spare chair which was at the far end. I quickly sat in it as Principal Williams sat down behind his desk.

"These guys are failing in math. Reese is a

whiz and it's been proven students learn better from other students, rather than private tutors."

Howard choked, "Well, my parents are paying good money for tutoring. If you're going to say what I think you're going to suggest, then I don't need it. I'll do more sessions with my own tutor."

Principal Williams rose an eyebrow, and his receding hairline glistened in the light as he smiled at me.

"You're having three sessions a week, and you've managed to only score 10% more than you did on the last quiz. Your tutor's not helping. You're all sporting experts, but not math experts."

He crossed his arms, and I felt as if I was being sucked into a dark hole as the three guys looked at me. I shifted uncomfortably in the leather chair, and turned to face away from them. I was hoping I wouldn't feel their stares. It wasn't the case, but I could dream the speech Principal Williams had planned would come to an end.

"I need to get the scholarship so I can get into college. My family depends on me," Alan said to Principal Williams.

Principal Williams nodded his head as if he was in agreement with him.

"I don't know what you have against her. But I do know one thing, she can help us, so if that's the case. I'm in!" Alan shrugged before slouching back in his seat, as if he was agreeing to be tutored one hundred percent.

He looked for confirmation from his BFF, who turned to get up, as if the suggestion from his friend annoyed him.

"I can't afford a damn tutor, and judging by your shit grades. I can say he's not doing a good job."

"She," Howard corrected Alan.

"She…" Alan murmured as if it would make things any better. Correcting and letting him know his tutor was female, instead of a male.

I sat as quiet as a mouse as Jeff spat out. "I'm easy. I need out of high school and in baseball."

I was scared to look his way, he only spoke kindly to others who were on the same level as him, which were others in sports or graced with good looks such as him with his emerald eyes and dark hair from his Italian heritage.

"Boys. Leave us. You can argue and accept this proposal, but it seems Reese is not game."

"Good!" Howard spat out, as he turned on the balls of his feet and walked out of the door.

Alan paused before sitting up, and then gave me a sympathetic smile, as if he wanted to say something, but didn't know how to phrase it.

Jeff ignored me, and headed out too.

As soon as the door was closed, I felt as if I

had been holding in my breath the entire time. I let out a deep sigh, releasing the anxiousness as I did it.

"I saw SCH and what Jade did. It wasn't nice. Your dad says you've been quiet lately. More quiet than usual."

I could feel his blue eyes staring at me, but I avoided them as I played with the rim of my black skirt.

"I want you to do this, to show them there's more to you and to maybe finish high school with a smile."

My head shot up, as if to defend myself.

"It's SC or Snapchat."

He giggled, "Yeah, you know I'm not good at these acronyms."

I nodded my head. "These guys will respect you and maybe you would be able to talk to someone in high school apart from me and your teachers."

I shook my head. "That's not fair. All they do is make fun of me."

He sighed, "T. That's not true. You know you don't let them get close to you. You were good friends with Hayley last year."

"And then Jade started posting some crap about her, and I knew it was because of me, so I just kept my distance."

He was about to say something, but then the bell rang, and it was time for me to go to another class.

"You can't let Jade walk all over you."

I nodded, thinking it was too late for that. It was what she'd done from the moment I joined high school, and why I'd put on thirty pounds and had no friends. Well, I couldn't blame her for everything. I'd eaten alone, but she made me feel this way and loneliness shadowed me as Principal Williams tried to smile and encourage me as I left his office.

I had to go to class, and I knew sooner or later I would face the boys. But before then I would go to the bathroom and have some candy. It always made me feel a little better. I needed it more than ever right now.

Reese

I'd managed to avoid seeing any one of them during the day, and part of me wondered if they were avoiding me. That was until I approached my car and saw not only Jeff, but Alan and Howard, too. All standing like lost puppies, clearly waiting for me to show up.

I held up my head, unlike when I walked into Principal Williams' office, not allowing them to intimidate me again. They couldn't if they tried, not the way I was feeling. I had a bad day, no a shit one. Not only did I get called into the Principal's office to be asked to tutor the boys, but then I found out something worse. I loved science, it was the passion which drove Jade and I together at such a young age. Now, she pretended or maybe it wasn't pretense that maybe she didn't love it like she used to do, but I studied it for fun. Something no one should ever admit in high school. Somehow I'd even lost the passion in something I desired so much that now I was failing, well not failing but my grades were not as they used to be and it hurt so bad.

It was as if something Principal Williams had said started to make sense in that there was something going on with me, so deep everyone on the outside could see it. Everyone but me.

"Slow down, Reese. We just want to talk," Alan said as he grabbed my arm. I did a full circle trying to avoid them, thinking drama was the last thing I needed to happen today.

Home.

B&J Brownie.

One tub or two, was the only thing on my mind as I faced him. Alan had never been cruel to me, he'd been nothing up until this day, yet here I was having to respond to him.

I decided against the latter as I tugged at my arm, trying to pull it away from him.

"We just want to talk," Jeff said with so much arrogance, as if it pained him to tell me he wanted to talk.

"We need your help."

Howard said it as if that was enough to make me stop doing whatever I was thinking of doing and do whatever they wanted me to do.

"Fuck you!" I spat out. They made my life a living hell, and now because they needed me, I should let it all be gone and do whatever they said? Not a chance.

"Wow, you've got some fighting spirit!" Jeff chuckled, and I moved towards him, wanting to let go of all my anger on him as I threw my bag onto the ground and launched at him.

Someone held me back, as I didn't do anything that was in my head. Instead all I managed to do was drop my bag on the ground while Alan held both my arms back. I struggled and clearly was no match for him. Howard walked slowly in front of me.

Did no one see what was going on?

No one to come to my aid?

Then again, they wouldn't because the three guys ran the school and were in charge, and silly me always parked in the spot at the corner of the school, which was away from everyone, but I knew they had to know where it was, and that my car was there.

I had this messed up idea out of sight meant out of mind, so if they didn't see me arrive and leave school every day maybe just once they would forget about me.

I began to sob, "Let go of me!"

As he held on to me even tighter, I knew my cries and trying to wrestle him didn't change a thing as I could feel his biceps tighten against me like a cobra. But, it didn't stop me from trying, it didn't stop me from putting up a fight. Maybe it was me finding out I was scoring low in science that made me put up a fight, yet it surprised me. I never knew I had this much drive, or that the little I used to have in me was dead.

"Wow, you're a fighter," Howard chuckled, and it just made me squirm even more. I was even more annoyed as he mocked me.

"Fuck you!"

"Shit, Jeff, it must be all the crap you give her, which is making her turn into a tough girl."

As they laughed, and as I faced Jeff who was pointing at me, I did something even more out of character.

I spat at him.

I gathered as much spit as I had and sent it in his direction. He jumped out of the way avoiding it. Alan let me go. No more were they laughing at me, but instead were in shock.

"Damn, Reese. I didn't. I mean we didn't. This isn't going the way we planned." Alan stuttered, letting me know as he moved away from me, and I slowly reached for my bag.

"There's three of you. And there's only me. I mean don't you think I'm tired of this shit. Each and every day. Being laughed at and then you hold me down and think I should listen to you like I'm one of the guys."

"We only wanted to apologize for how we behaved in Principal Williams' office and to ask if you would consider tutoring us."

Jeff being nice? Before I bent down, I spun my head around to see if my ears were deceiving me. They weren't.

"We don't deserve your support. I mean you're rich, an excellent student, you volunteer and you're in nearly every club in school…"

"I was," I muttered, thinking about how my life at high school had started and how it was now. Now, I had nothing to get me into Stanford, apart from the extra credit I could get from tutoring them. I didn't care, I just wanted out of there. Away from them.

"We would like you to think about it. We don't say we deserve it."

I moved away from my bag, and headed towards Howard.

"You don't deserve it. You're fucking right. You and your precious girlfriend have made my life a living hell being here."

He nodded his head.

I couldn't retain my resentment to this agreement any longer, as I blurted out, "You would be the last person I would tutor. You deserve to fail."

He blinked as I said it, which probably surprised him, as much as it had surprised myself saying something so nasty. Nasty wasn't in me. I'd heard, and been a recipient to horrible comments for so long, I wondered as if it was starting to be drilled inside of me.

I felt scared at the whole idea of being someone I really wasn't. So I swiftly grabbed my bag and then moved to my car. I didn't need them. I had to figure out a way to get the extra credits when I wasn't feeling so emotional.

A hand grabbed the car door as I clicked the button on the key.

"There must be something we can do," Alan begged, as my eyes met his and I could see he was pleading with me.

"I dare you all to take me to the fucking Valentine's Dance!"

I blurted it out and didn't wait for them to

reply, as I sat down in the car, and he slammed the door shut. I turned the engine and moved out of my space. My eyes flashed up to see their faces; they all had blank expressions, and for a split second I wondered if they were thinking about it.

Nah!

They wouldn't dream of it.

Then again, Alan was so desperate to get into college maybe he would do it but as for the rest, they wouldn't, not in a million years.

⁓

*T*ears were streaming down from my eyes as I drove home. I paused for a second as I reached the gate, then decided to drive on. I could hear my phone chiming, meaning someone had left a message, or maybe it was more than one, because it kept beeping and I had no idea who could be calling. Either it was my absent father who spent more time on business trips than he did in the house, or my mom who did the same, but mainly in the country club.

No one was at home, apart from Josephine who was the housekeeper, and today was her day off. Therefore, no one cared if I was there or not. I passed my house and decided to keep on driving.

I drove to the Rock in the Mountains Reserve, near where I lived to go to a place I used to find sanctuary with Nan when she was alive. The place I could go and all my troubles felt as if they disappeared. I parked the car, and as I got out, a cool breeze greeted me, keeping me cool. I smiled and took my bag, then looked at my phone.

I'm sorry for the past. Can we start again? You've got a deal. Howard

We need your help. Understand if you don't want to, but I know I don't deserve a second chance if you can forgive the past, then I would appreciate it. Jeff

I really need your help. Please can you consider tutoring us. Alan

The three of them were willing to go through with it. I didn't know whether to be happy or sad about the idea of going to the dance with them. Something I'd never thought I would be doing, or be given an opportunity to do it. It was one thing wanting something to happen, and another having it take place. I was scared, frightened about the idea of it but excited at the same time. Howard would have to tell Jade, and I wish I could be a fly on the wall to see the look on her face.

lan

There was so much pressure on me. From playing in the game, to making sure I got into college on scholarship. It was a dream my single mom with three kids had had since, I could remember. She'd sacrificed a lot and I felt as if I owed her. It wasn't fair for me to think of doing anything else in my life, but paying it forward.

I was to meet Reese in the library. I was so fucking nervous. She didn't know, only Howard did, that I was shit at algebra. So shit that on the last quiz, I cheated and still failed because I couldn't even make out my cheat notes.

Being tutored by someone as smart as Reese just made me feel nervous. She would find out how crap I was and how much work it would take to even just pass, and probably bail out of tutoring me altogether. I wouldn't blame her. She suggested we have individual sessions so she would know our level and would know how to work best with us. I'd managed to book a quiet room at the corner of the library so we could at least talk.

"Sorry, I'm late," she smiled with her face all flustered as if she'd been running. Her dark hair was a mess, but then it was so curly and long, I had a feeling it was a pain to brush every morning. I hadn't seen her all day at school, so I wondered if she would even show up today.

"It's ok. I finished training early, so I thought I would come straight here."

She nodded as she dumped her bag on the side chair, and then sat next to me.

Her strong perfume tickled my nose, and I couldn't help but sneeze as she came close, pushing a folder my way.

"You okay?"

I nodded. "Yeah, just allergies. They mess with me sometimes."

She looked at me strangely with her brows crossed and her dark eyes staring at me, as if she was waiting for me to say something else.

I placed my hand on hers to reassure her.

"I've never stuck up for you, but I've never been cruel either."

She shrugged, "As if silence was a remedy for being innocent."

She was right. If I sat back and watched someone carry out a crime, it wouldn't make me innocent. No, I would be deemed an accomplice. I knew it, and so did she. I shouldn't be defending my shitty attitude in the past, I should be apologizing for it.

"Sorry," I purred as I took her hand, so she faced me. I couldn't take all this negative energy, especially when I was trying to play down my role in her bullying. I'd watched as Jade put up the fake underwear, and put it up for everyone to see, did nothing as Jade distracted her one time, and put enough bicarbonate soda, in which Reese is allergic to in large doses to make Reese have a bad reaction which resulted in her face being covered in spots. The first day the reaction took place she left school, and missed a whole week after .

Sure, I hadn't taken an active role, but it didn't

mean I was completely innocent as she'd pointed out.

"The only thing I can do is apologize."

She nodded, but then she turned her head to face me. Her light brown eyes shined, and it was the first time I'd taken in her beauty. I'd never looked at her in this way before. Not until now.

"All I can do is apologize and say I was wrong in the past, but I'm trying to do better in the future."

She ignored my comment as she shoved the papers in front of me. Then she told me to take the short quiz she'd constructed to find out my weaknesses, and the best way for her to go forward.

I looked at the papers as if they were in a foreign language. I'd spent most of the night studying for it, but I didn't have a clue how to approach it. I knew right then, she would probably mock me when she saw how bad I was at algebra.

I was bad.

Really fucking bad.

*R*eese asked for us to leave the library, it was getting late and what should have been an hour session had turned into two.

"If we spend any more time in the library, then we would need a sleeping bag."

I sighed, "Yeah, I should have warned you about my struggles."

She gathered the papers and motioned for us to leave. As she stood up, she quickly pulled up her jeans which had fallen. Then she turned red, as if she was embarrassed about me seeing her exposed panties. I must admit, it did get me curious. I thought she would have some plain cotton panties, not some silky black number with red hearts over it. My cock jerked at the sight of it, luckily she couldn't see I was flushed, but if I thought about it any longer then she'd know I was getting hard.

I followed her like a duck to water as she left the library and held open the door for her, like a true gentleman. She passed by me, and once again the vision of her panties and her straw-berry scented shampoo made me horny.

"Hit me with it!"

She giggled, "It's not bad. I mean I was watching you as you were tackling the problems and I saw you working it out and I know what your problem is."

"Apart from I suck at math."

She shook her head. "I thought you were an athlete. I thought you were supposed to have confidence in everything you did, and any obstacle was seen as a challenge."

I took in a deep breath, knowing only my one best friend, Howard, knew the truth about my home life. No one else did, and no one asked, which was fine by me.

When you're semi-popular in high school, then no one's digging up your past. They're too busy trying to be seen with you, and have you as a friend rather than an enemy.

As we stood by her black Audi RS Q8, I paused, thinking the price of her car was more than how much the apartment was mom was renting in Resort-Style Portofino Community.

"This baby has some speed. Do you take it up the mountains a-lot? Especially because your house is near the preserve?"

She shook her head, as if I'd said something to offend her.

"No. Why? You've seen me there?"

I smoothed my hand over the shining front, and then door, wondering if one day I could afford a car as luxurious as this.

"Nah, I'm just thinking that up there you can really do some rides and it would be fun, is all."

"Yeah, if I had someone to share it with, then maybe it would be fun."

She opened the back door and stuffed her books at the back with her bag, and then stood in front of me. It was then it hit me. I thought if you had money, then you had happiness. The little time I'd spent with Reese she appeared to be lonely, or maybe she was just nervous like I felt being around her.

"I thought you would mock me. Make fun of the fact my math is so bad. I mean, it's horrible."

"I'm bullied enough. I know what it's like to be ridiculed. I wouldn't do that to you. Besides, your problem isn't that it's impossible for you. You just over-complicate things. There's always a clue. A part that makes everything fall into place, so we'll start our next session by concentrating on just how to make it simpler. Okay?"

"You're not bad Reese, not bad at all," I purred as I moved closer to her, and then gave her a kiss on the cheek.

I expected her to flinch or move back, but she didn't. She made me feel good about something I didn't think was possible. I felt as if I could jump in her car and drive up the mountains. Like I told her, it would be a fun ride, but I couldn't. I didn't have a license, I couldn't afford the sessions.

It was as if she was welcoming me, as I jerked my head back slightly, and moved my lips to hers. They trembled as I put my full lips on her oval shaped mouth. I pulled her closer towards me, and I could feel the tension she once had start to melt away. I didn't know how long we'd held the kiss, but I decided to release her.

She looked down, a bright shade of red as I did it.

"You didn't need to do that."

She reached for the car door.

I held on to it. "I didn't. But I wanted to."

She gave me a quizzical look again, as if she was trying to figure me out. I had a hard on, and between her car which I found sexy, and her panties flashing through my mind, I knew if we stayed in the parked car any longer I would have her bent over her car and taking her from behind. I moved away, and she smiled at me. I watched as she closed the door, and touched her lips. She'd never been kissed before. I waved as I walked away feeling good about myself, knowing I'd done the right thing by being tutored by her, and wanting to get close and personal too.

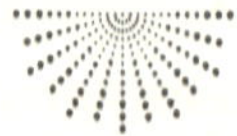

CHAPTER THREE

*J*eff

J invited Reese to my house for a first session. Alan had said he'd seen noticeable changes in the time he'd been studying and he'd only had three sessions with her. Three long sessions; I wondered if they were really studying or doing something else.

"Do you want something to drink?"

Reese shook her head as Maria, the housekeeper, brought her in to the study. She was wearing a pale green dress that made her eyes shine. Her hair was tied back, and she was dressed completely different to how she was at school. She wasn't wearing a big shirt which covered her body, but a dress which emphasized her curves. I liked the change, but decided there was no way she was wearing it just for our session. It was the weekend, maybe she had plans afterwards.

"I just want us to get on with it."

I deserved that. I'd been a jerk to her throughout high school, but we couldn't have a good session, not when she was so uptight.

"I know we didn't see eye-to-eye in the past…"

Before I could even get another word out, she crossed her arms, letting me know she wasn't happy to be here, not one bit.

"Seeing eye-to-eye would imply we had a disagreement of some kind. Not the fact you made me feel like shit every time I went to the cafeteria. Which was why now, I bring food in from home, and eat anywhere there is no one else, which sometimes includes the bathroom cubicle."

It was as if her confession had embarrassed her, but she didn't realize it made me feel a lot worse.

"I'm sorry. Really? The bathroom?"

She shrugged, "Well, where else could I go?"

I didn't have a list of places one could go on the school ground to avoid jerks. So, I assumed she had figured out places to eat and had found a sanctuary.

I drew closer to her.

"So, what do you do when someone comes in and does a dump?"

"Run!"

We both laughed at the same time as she said it. She had unfolded her arms, so I knew she was a little more relaxed, but not entirely.

"I love being the center of attention."

"At my expense."

I shook my head, knowing she got it all wrong. "No. At anyone's expense, and you're an easy target. My parents have money, but compared to yours, it's pennies."

"Is that what all this is about? Money? What about feelings? What about making someone feel as if they're worth something."

Before I could open my mouth, the one person I hated more than myself at the time, walked into the room.

My dad.

"So, you're Reese Smith. I see you've come to help my son who clearly didn't take after me in the gene pool with his math."

She spun around to face him. As usual, he was

dressed in a tux. Sometimes I wondered if he wore the damn thing to bed. He spent more time looking as if he was going to a ball than he did to the office.

"Yes, sir."

He chuckled, "Anyone as smart as you can call me Damon. Yet, I feel you're wasting your time."

Her eyes darted to mine, which then moved to the floor. I didn't want to see or even hear what he had to say about the matter.

"We need a priest or even better, Jesus, to try and get this one to pass math. I'm even surprised he has average grades in his other subjects. He needs a miracle, not a tutor. Anyway, if you have free time and nothing to do on a Saturday then attempt to make a difference."

"Jeffrey!" He barked at me.

"Yes, sir."

"Make sure Reese is well looked after and if your mother can attempt to get out of bed, then let her know I've left for my trip to London."

I replied, "Of course, sir."

The smile Reese had greeted him with, disappeared as he spun around and left the room. We didn't exchange words, but I was frozen in the spot, ashamed for her to see the life I led. Most of the time when I invited my friends over, I made sure they came over whenever he wasn't around. When

Reese said to have the session at my house, I'd forgotten there was a slim chance he would be here.

"You call your dad sir?"

I ignored her, and it was as if I had a rude awakening, and wanted to bypass the embarrassment of what had just taken place as I cleared my throat, trying to find the voice I'd lost after he walked into the room.

"Let's go to the study!"

Dad may come back in here, and the only place he never really ventured in, was the study and mom's bedroom. The two places he knew she could be in, if she was in the house.

~

We'd been studying for well over a couple of hours, the scene with my dad had become a thing of the past, and talking too. I soon realized we had a lot more in common than I realized.

"One more year til the finale of Stranger Things, so who do you think is on the hit list?" I quizzed as she told me some theories about the series. Things I'd never considered.

"Max needs to die. The crazy thing is at the moment it's gone way past the original story. No more is it about the end of the world, there's the whole theory about Steve and his six nuggets, then the love triangle with Johnny. Harper finally finding love, and the Russians."

I lifted my hand, "Yeah, the Russian thing threw me. It was like, how many storylines can you fit into one series?"

"Maybe they'll make spin-offs."

"Then spin-offs of the spin-offs!"

We both chuckled as I said the last thing.

"I can't believe you played Dungeons & Dragons with Jade when you were younger."

The smile she had on her face disappeared. "Yeah, and a couple of other girls who both moved away, and then it was just Jade and me, then high school, and well you know the rest."

A tear appeared in her eye, as if talking about Jade and high school had set her off. My instincts kicked in and I gently wiped the tear from her face and pushed a lock of her hair back behind her ear. Even when she was upset and weepy, she was gorgeous.

Like Jade, I'd caused Reese to experience emotional pain. I knew it, and I'd even been in the same situation many times with my dad, yet I still had done it to her and many others. It was as if it made me feel better, feel as if I was superior to someone, since dad had always made me feel like I was a piece of shit.

I watched as she sank back into the couch next to me. She leaned her head back, and closed her eyes. The stress and worry was etched deep into her face. I gently ran my finger across her temple and down her cheek. I wanted nothing more than to see her face free from pain.

"Reese," I said softly, looking down at her. She opened her eyes and her gaze met mine.

"I shouldn't have been a shit to you."

She gave a slight nod and a brief smile.

"Especially because your dad does the same to you. And your mom?"

"Drunk," I blurted, as I scooped her up into a body-squeezing hug. We were no longer sitting, as we stood there like for a few minutes, just holding each other.

I could tell my actions surprised her, because it was out of the blue. She'd made me feel better about myself in such a short space of time. I felt her nuzzle her head a little further into my shoul-der. Unable to stop myself, I slowly started running my hand through her hair. It felt so good just to hold her. I could feel her breathing against me, the rise and fall of her chest sending her breasts pushing into me. I tried to control myself as I continued to trace my fingers up and down her spine. I felt her shiver and heard her giggle as she looked up at me.

"That tickled." I laughed as I looked down at her, still pressed close to me. She wrapped her arms around my waist before looking into my eyes.

"You can't treat people bad to compensate for your dad. It's not right and it's not fair."

"I know."

I leaned forward, and she didn't back away. Instead, she met me halfway and we found ourselves tangled in each other's arms, our lips locked together in fiery passion.

As our tongues danced together, I could feel myself growing hard. Feeling her hands on my shoulders, digging in, turned me on to a point where I didn't want it to stop. I picked her up and positioned her until she was straddling me as I carried her over to the couch. I wanted to taste her and to feel my cock sliding down her throat. I sat down with her on top of me but she didn't stay that way for long. She broke off our kiss, panting, and stepped back to face me. One by one, I watched her as she let each article of clothing fall to the floor at my feet. My heart was beating out of my chest as I drank in the sight of her.

Her rosy nipples were begging for me

to suck them as she proudly showed off her perfect, perky breasts and tightly toned body. I reached out to touch her, only to have my hand playfully swatted away. As she came forward, she dropped to her knees and her fingers found my belt buckle. I drew in a sharp breath as she skillfully pulled me out from my pants and drew the length of me into her mouth. I could barely concentrate. The way her tongue moved in little circles along my shaft had shivers coursing through my body. I reached down and tangled my hands in her hair, slowly testing just how much of me she could take. I was not disappointed. Not wanting her to stop but also not wanting to embarrass myself for anything happening sooner than it should, I pulled her up, stood up, and threw her down on to the couch so she was laying where I had just been sitting. I pulled off my shirt and threw it aside and saw her seductive smile begging for me.

"Are you sure you want to do this?"

She panted, "Do you have a rubber?"

Her question surprised me. I thought she would back away, not want to get down and dirty in the library. I did have a condom. I was a creature of habit, and always carried one with me. I took it from my back pocket, and then used my teeth to undo the wrapper and set it free.

With one hand, I took her wrists and pinned them on the arm of the couch above her head, teasing her breasts with my other hand, lightly running my fingers around each nipple and caressing each voluptuous breast before slowly, lazily, trailing my fingers down her stomach to her pelvic line. A fire lit behind her eyes as I eased her legs apart to find her already wet and ready for me to take her. I locked my eyes on hers as I slid a finger inside her, then two. She was so tight. I watched as her body writhed beneath my touch, fingering her faster and faster until I felt her muscles begin to tighten. I wanted this time to last but knew both of us were so ready to just explode. I flipped her over on the couch so her perfect little ass was pointing up towards me and I climbed on top of her. Pinning her hands behind her back, I positioned myself to be angled right over her, I used one hand to slide on the rubber, while keeping her still and slowly sliding my throbbing cock deep into her.

I worked hard to control myself as I heard her moans and felt her match my rhythm. Releasing her arms, I positioned myself even further, nearly laying on top of her, allowing me to reach even deeper. I began fucking her faster, harder; her body matching mine move for move; her screams growing louder as I brought her to the peak of ecstasy. I felt her muscles squeezing, making her feel even tighter around me. Neither of us could withhold any longer and with one deep thrust, I felt her cum all over my cock pushing me to the breaking point.

We were making a lot of noise, but I knew no one in the house would dare come into the study. The door was locked, and although I hated the way I took her so fast and furious, the excitement of it all got too much for me.

"We should get cleaned up. Let's go up to my room."

She turned to face me, her face red and hot from the session we'd just had, and I could tell she was uncomfortable with what had just taken place.

"I was a virgin," she whispered.

I shook my head in disbelief, because for sure, I must have hurt her. Something I didn't want to do. I needed to put the way I treated her before at the back of my mind, and do better by her.

"Oh no. You were screaming out of pain and not pleasure. Shit!"

She held on to my hand, and said, "It's ok. I just didn't know it was going to be like that."

I smiled, "Look, let's go to my room. Not only to get you cleaned up, but to do it again."

"Again?"

I grinned, "The way I should have done it. Especially for your first time."

She pulled up her panties, and I got rid of the condom by sliding it into my back pocket. I had some more rubbers in my room. If she did wear the dress to go somewhere today then there was no point, all her plans had been canceled because she was spending today and possibly the night with me. I wanted to make love to her the way I should have done, especially because it was her first time.

CHAPTER FOUR

*R*eese

The last few days had been nuts, I'd gone from not having any attention to, too much attention. Howard had not booked a session with me, and to tell you the truth I was glad for it.

I'd gone in the space of two weeks from being a virgin, to not only sleeping with one jock but two. A part of me was like it is all going to end horribly. Jade hadn't been at school all week, which made me feel as if I had a new lease in life. I didn't have to worry about her, and for some reason the new attention I'd been seeking felt warranted, as if I deserved it after all these years of being treated like a shit in high school.

"Hey, you want to come sit with us at lunch?" Aaliyah asked. She was Alan's twin, and somehow seeing us together made us friends. I'd always admired her swag.

"Sure, I really love your new dress."

She twirled around showing me her bright, yellow dress which was mid-length and had thin straps, and some kind of orange African design in the middle of it.

"Yeah, made it myself. Took me a week, but I'm proud of it. Fashion school, here I come after being locked up in this high school for too long."

I walked with her as we approached the cafeteria. It was a place I used to hate so much but now it seemed to be a thing of the past. No more fear. I didn't think this new confidence would ever exist in me.

"There's no way I could wear a summer dress in winter," I sighed as I admired her dress. Underneath the dress, she wore an orange polo to no doubt match the African design in the middle of the dress. The cut was perfect. I'd been to one too many designer stores when my mom wanted me to be like her. The perfect child, with the perfect mom until I started putting on weight and no more did she want to be seen with me. In fact, it was the complete opposite as she kept telling me I was an embarrassment to her.

"You know I could make something for you, if you like. It's just I know you like dark colors and I don't do dark."

I chuckled as she spun around again, and she giggled as if to let me know her taste.

"I know. You've even got orange in your bungie. Yep, you love color and I wear dark, because they say it makes you look thinner."

"Child! There's nothing wrong with your body. You are what you feel. You need to come to my house. All my family does is feed you. Especially when Nan's in town, which she is at the moment. Don't let no one make you feel any less than you already are."

I nodded my head, but it was easy for her to say. I couldn't tell her the one person that made me feel this way was my own mother.

"But, what about Alan?"

"What about him?" She quizzed as we reached the cafeteria doors.

"He may mind me coming to your house."

She shook her head and encouraged me to join the queue, which was ever increasing as students lined up to eat.

"No silly, it was his idea."

She surprised me by her words because I

remember one time Alan saying he never invited anyone to his house. I never asked why and he never offered any information about it. The idea he wanted me there made me feel special, something which I never thought was possible for someone like me.

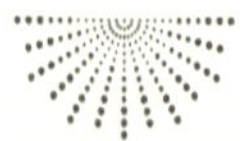

Howard

I hadn't booked a session with Reese because when I told Jade about it, she flipped out. I noticed both Jeff and Alan had been hanging out with her, and I felt jealous. Not only because their grades were improving in the short space of time, but they were hanging out with her.

It was as if in the last two weeks she had completely changed. The idea of taking her to the Valentine's dance wasn't something I was open to at first, but now I was having second thoughts.

"Stop staring at her like that. It's fucking

creepy!" Alan said as he waved to Reese who was sitting on the bench watching us train. Something she'd never done in the past, but he said today they would go to his house to have dinner.

"You've never invited me to your house for dinner. How come Reese gets to go."

He shrugged, "Your bedroom is the size of my damn apartment which I share with mom and my sisters. Dunno. I just didn't feel comfortable doing it. You can come if you like? Nan always cooks too much."

I liked his Nan, she'd been to a few games when she'd come here from New Orleans. She always invited me, and Alan always said I was busy. He would never give me a chance to respond.

"And Reese's house is double the size of mine. So, I don't get it."

"Shit, chill. If it means that much to you, then you can come along."

"So, I could be the third-wheel," I grunted.

He shook his head. "I can't fucking win with you man. One minute you want to come and the next you don't. Fuck it!" He gave me his back then headed towards the lockers. No doubt to get changed and showered.

Now, I wasn't the only one looking at someone weirdly, Reese was doing the same to me. Then she jumped up, and headed up the stairs.

Jade's words were going around in my head. She'd been home the last two weeks after breaking her arm one night when she was drunk. That was what she said, but even I didn't believe her.

There was a rumor one the guys was trying to keep quiet from me. One which had involved her seeing another senior from the high school downtown. I didn't want to believe it, but I knew Jade better than most and I knew lies flew out of her mouth like forest fires spreading on a hot day. I'd witnessed her say them one too many times without a second thought or even caring about their consequences.

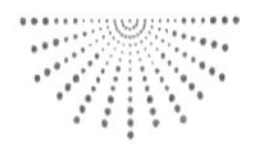

CHAPTER SIX

Reese

I went a little overboard when I went to Alan's. I wore a red dress Aaliyah made for me. She said I had to show my curves and stop pretending they didn't exist.

Even Maria said I looked beautiful this morning as I left home. Beautiful and me, didn't seem right in the same sentence. But I tied my hair up in a bun, and everyone, and even a couple of teachers, said I looked nice. Principal Williams as I passed him in the hallway, made it known by a secret wink he thought I looked good today.

It was weird. I'd gone from the last couple of weeks hiding from everyone, to now being the main attention. A lot of people apologized to me, it was as if Jade not being around made everyone feel more relaxed, including me. But she was due to come back to school tomorrow and I was scared things may change. They may go back to the way they were before, but there was a part of me that didn't care.

The part which relished in how I was feeling at the moment and just enjoying it for now.

"Child, you need to fill your plate again. No one leaves this table until it's all gone. You hear me?" Nana beamed from the other side of the table.

"Having a family meal is something I haven't had in a long time."

"Why?" She asked with a concerned look on her face.

"Well, the only time I had it was when my Nan was alive, and she passed a couple of years ago."

She nodded. "I see."

I didn't get what she saw, but then Alan's mom completely changed the conversation and what I'd turned into a sad moment was quickly turned back to the way it was before I talked about Nan.

"Nana, if we all keep eating like this, then we're gonna get stuck here!"

I chuckled at the way Alan's speech changed when he was with his family. He didn't talk like at school, but being with his family they all spoke the same way, and I loved it.

Mom would have a heart attack if she saw how much I was eating, but I didn't care. I could hear my phone beeping in my bag which hung on the chair.

I took it out, and there before me was a message that I really wasn't expecting, and it sent cold shivers down my spine.

I need your help. I know I didn't agree to the dance, and I don't deserve it. But if we can have a math session on Sunday at 2 at my house. I would be forever be in your debt.

*H*oward

. . .

BTW, this means yes, I will take you to the dance.

Howard

That's if you would tutor me. I hope it's a yes.

Howard

"No phones at the table!" Nana screamed as I scrolled through not one message, but a few where Howard clearly was as nervous as I was about tutoring him.

"You all right?" Alan asked, as his hand touched mine.

. . .

I nodded my head, unable to speak. I wondered if he knew Howard was going to send me a message. Either way, I had turkey, cornbread and some greens being pilled on my plate, a mission which I had to accomplish. I was happy the dress didn't hug me as tightly as a second skin, because by the time I finished my plate, one thing I was confident about, it would.

CHAPTER SEVEN

H oward

R eese replied, and I felt like some lovesick horny teenager as I prepared for my first tuition session with Reese.

"Well, I think Jade will be really impressed with the efforts you've made today." Mom kissed me on the cheek, and her and dad then prepared for another church event. At times, it was as if they spent more time there than anywhere else. Dad had a cancer scare a year back and since then they've been at the church's beck and call. Prayers and healing cured him. Never mind the doctors and the big fat cheque they received once he was out of remission. It was a crap time for all of us. Jade's support included telling me I was becoming boring and she would have to look for a new beau. This was when I suspected she ran into the arms of another, but I didn't care. I was on one prayer crusade after another with my parents and apart from that, I was thankful he had survived and my parents who used to ignore me, all of a sudden remembered I existed, and even better, they began to care.

"Mom, I told you I have a math session, and I'm breaking up with Jade."

My dad cleared his throat, his cue to tell mom to mind her own business, whenever she asked me about matters of the heart.

"If that's true son, then you can have any new car you want. No price is the limit. Hallelujah, my prayers have been answered!"

Mom fake slapped him. Dad made no secret of his dislike of Jade.

You should be seeing good girls. Girls on your level. Not girls like Jade.

He'd said it one too many times. I never knew what he meant, until dad got sick and I saw the side of her somehow dad had seen from the start. We'd been dating since the first year of high school. He was polite to her, that part was for sure, but as soon as he got the chance, he would remind me Jade was not the girl for me.

Mom on the other hand, loved the idea of me having a childhood sweetheart. Dad had been hers and she'd voiced one too many times high school was the best place to meet your soulmate.

"Anyway, have fun."

I didn't say anything as she waved and then headed out of the door. I told her I had a math session, and she was telling me to have fun. It made no sense at all, neither did mom most of the time, but I still loved her.

I'd been plotting around the house, at least three times. Wondering if Reese had stood me up, then reminding myself it wasn't a date. I even changed my polo a couple of times. I'd gone from my sky blue one, which mom said matched my eyes to my grey one, which I felt made me look as if I worked at the country club.

Either way, clothes weren't really my thing. I tended to wear anything that made me feel comfortable, but Jade constantly complained I had no sense of style. Then again, she complained all the time about anything I did, which made no sense why we were even together.

I heard the doorbell ring, and I rushed down. I was getting anxious and annoyed about all my energy taken up thinking about Jade.

"Hey," I said as I opened the door.

She hesitated as she hugged her wool coat over her body. Her hair was tied up, something I noticed she'd been doing a lot lately but her face didn't return my smile.

"Is Jade here?"

"No," I chuckled nervously.

"It's just when you sent the message, I thought maybe you were up to something, so Aaliyah came with me."

That was when I noticed the reason why she kept looking to her right, instead of facing me.

"Hey, Howie. I just wanted to make sure my girl was okay."

She nodded as if to justify her actions. Part of me was disappointed by her assumption, then again I didn't blame her. I would have done the same if I was in her position. I wouldn't think any less of me neither.

"Hey, Aaliyah. You want to come in?"

She shook her head, and then I noticed both Aaliyah and Reese locking arms, and the one thing Jade said could never happen, had been done. Reese after all this time had a friend, even if it was under the worst circumstance.

"Jade's not here. It's not a prank, so you don't need to worry."

They both exchanged a look, and then looked back at me.

"Please don't tell Alan, he doesn't know I'm here."

I nodded to confirm what I'd already suspected, Alan didn't know they thought it was a prank, and they were both here.

"Right, so I'll be on my way then," Aaliyah said as she broke away from Reese.

Reese looked lost as Aaliyah hugged her, whispered something in her ear and then turned to walk away. She froze, as if she didn't know whether to come in or leave herself.

I broke the ice as I held on to the door and asked her to come in.

"I promise I won't bite."

She had a nervous smile on her face, and said nothing as she walked past me to the hallway. I was nervous about her coming around, but it seems she was a lot more nervous than I was about this whole thing.

"Why did you change your mind?" She asked as she spun around to face me.

"Why did you decide you now need sessions? It's like you didn't want them before and now all of a sudden, you're so willing!"

She crossed her arms and held on to her coat even tighter. It hit me, like a fucking tornado, she wasn't waiting for Jade to show up, but for me to do something cruel to her.

"I've seen how Jeff and Alan's grades have transformed overnight and I know it all comes down to you."

"And?" She barked this time, while squinting her eyes as if she wanted me to say something else. There was some other reason to do this.

"It's not like you would take me to the dance. After all, your reputation and your relationship with the love of your life would be in shatters if you do."

I choked and laughed as she said it. It was funny her thinking of Jade as the love of my life.

I walked past her and headed to the kitchen. I felt like a soda to give me some energy. It was as if all the nerves of today had drained everything out of me, and I needed a sugar rush to give me some energy.

"Girlfriend. Fuck buddy. Dictator. But no way is she the love of my life."

Reese's heeled boots tapped behind me as she followed me.

"That's a little crude, considering how tight you both are."

I didn't answer as I opened the fridge and took out the first soda that caught my eye, Coke. I needed both the caffeine and sugar rush if it

meant getting Reese to sit down with me to talk,
let alone tutor me. I gave her a bottle, and she
took it. She surprised me because I wondered if I
gave her the wrong answer, would she be out the
door in a flash.

I took out the opener, and removed the lids as
we stood by the kitchen island. She took her
bottle and then started sipping on it like a lady,
while I grabbed the bottle, knocked my head back
and gulped it down as if my life depended on it.

"Better!" I said as I put the empty bottle on the
island.

"Everyone knows she's fucking some guy at
Phoenix Ridge, so please don't pretend she's the
love of my life."

She didn't say a word, and her eyes widened
as if I'd shocked her. It was as if all the blood had
been drained from her face as she became white
as a ghost.

"But you're still together."

I shrugged, and walked slowly behind her. I'd
heard both Jeff and Alan talk about what it was
like to be with Reese and part of me didn't want
to be tutored anymore. I just wanted what they'd
had and some more.

"You need to take your coat off. It's not cold in
here."

I put my hands over her shoulders and didn't

protest when I started to take off her coat. My curiosity wanted to see what she had on underneath it.

She wore a white ribbed polo and jeans with knee-high boots. I moved away from her, enjoying the view of every inch of her body.

She didn't face me, so she didn't see me put her coat on the stool beside me.

I moved towards her and stroked her back as if she was a delicate flower. Her hair was pinned up, and I gently moved my fingers so I could give wet kisses on her neck.

"I thought you wanted me here to study?" Her voice trembled as she spoke.

"I did, but you didn't bring any notes. Besides, I couldn't concentrate with your hot body driving me insane."

I spun her around, and then pulled up her sweater. She didn't stop me - she didn't even try, as I tossed it on the other side of the kitchen. Her lacy— bra didn't hide her hard nipples dying to be sucked. I moved my hand to the back of her bra and set them free.

"Beautiful," I growled, as I lifted up her breasts in my hands and started to massage them.

"Don't stop, please don't stop!"

With my one hand free, I undid her belt, and

then started to pull down her jeans along with her panties.

"Your parents, they could come back…"

"No!" I growled as I got the part of her I had been longing for: her pussy. It was wet and moist from my touch. I stroked the inside of her legs as she started to scream.

"Howard!"

My tongue enfolded her folds, making sure not to miss a piece. My dick was so fucking hard, wanting to exchange places with my tongue, but I had to hold off. I wanted to pleasure her. Not me.

She whimpered as I bit down slowly on her clit, but I knew I had to get her completely naked. There was a sense of urgency as I tugged on her jeans with her panties, and they were met with her boots.

Reese's hands were in my hair as she moaned loudly, and all I wanted to do was to make her scream. I held on to her legs which had started to move. I stopped for a brief second, but it felt like minutes as I took off her boots and jeans, so that she was butt naked in my kitchen.

All her curves and folds were on display, and I loved it. She had the body of a real woman, not just bones and padded bras. I lifted her up onto the island, then with my head in-between her legs, I started to get to work, one hand helping me keep in position, while the other played around her breasts. Every curve and taste of her sweet pussy was driving her insane as she screamed at the top of her lungs, leaving her sweet cum on the tip of my tongue.

I'd never been the type of guy to rip off Jade's clothes as soon as she walked through the door. I'd never had that desire or urge, yet there was something about Reese that made me want to do it. I backed away from her, leaving her sprawled on the island, trying to catch her breath. Once she did then she leaned up and smiled, "I hope I didn't taste bad."

My dick which was rock hard, felt as if it was being strangled, and dying to get out of my jeans.

"I need to go get freshened up," I struggled to say, and I didn't wait for her to reply as I headed up the stairs to my room so I could jerk off. I needed to get myself in check. I did ask her to come here so she could tutor me. Not to have my tongue fuck her pussy, even if it did taste so fucking good.

~

I called both Jeff and Alan to come over to my place. As soon as I jerked off and left my bathroom, Reese had left. I didn't blame her. I wasn't sure how long I was in there, but I did say to her I would be back soon. Who knows how long I was gone for? One thing for sure, I needed to find a new tutor. I hadn't even had a session with her, and I had her butt naked on my kitchen island.

"I hope this is important," Jeff barked as I opened the front door and they both walked in.

"Yeah. I need to be up early. Math is getting better, but you know how it goes. I finally under-stand algebra and Ms. Clark makes it more difficult."

I shut the door behind them, they were both wearing black which was a little weird, then again I did ask them to help me spy on Jade.

"You'll need this," Alan spun around and gave me a black hat with holes in it and then walked to the kitchen. He opened the fridge and took out a soda.

Jeff shook his head as I kept on looking at the hat.

"Don't ask. I said the same thing. How come he has this? You don't want to know the answer."

He was right, I didn't want to know. Some things were best left unsaid.

"So, we're going to the professor's house, right. I think his wife is out of town." Jeff said it so casually, I didn't know what to make of it.

Alan slammed the can on the island.

"Shit, he doesn't know man. I needed a drink to tell him."

Jeff shrugged, "How the fuck was I supposed to know he didn't know. I thought he knew and wanted some pictures or something."

I stood between them as if I was in the middle of a tennis match, and I had no idea what was going on as their voices raised and no one was filling me in.

"Can you please tell me what the fuck you're both talking about!" I screamed.

They both looked at me as if they were in shock, but then Jeff tilted his head to the side, to let me know it was Alan who had to speak. Alan who had to do the talking. After all, he was my best friend, and I wondered if he really was, as he started to tell me something, something I really didn't know.

"It's what you've been thinking Jade is cheating on you with some senior or student at Phoenix Ridge High, right?"

I didn't answer, because he knew the answer to the question.

"Well, it's not a student. It's a teacher."

"How do you know?"

He could be guessing, the same way I had.

"You were fucked up with your dad and

cancer and shit. And well, I knew. So, cause I haven't got a car, and I couldn't think who else to give me a ride who I could trust, I asked Jeff to stalk her. This is why we have the hats."

He was telling me what they did, and I had a feeling at the end of the story, I wasn't going to like. So, I grabbed a stool, since he was talking slowly, which meant he was choosing his words carefully.

"So, the first day nothing. The second day we saw her going downtown to some sleazy motel. We followed and waited until she came out and then…" Jeff said, filling in the gaps and waiting for Alan to fill in the rest.

"We saw her come out with some old guy. I was like holy shit, I recognized him. We had a game there once and he filled in for the coach, he was the History teacher or something like that. I don't remember those details, but it was her and it was definitely him."

Jeff slid his phone over to me, and they were in color, with Jade kissing the guy, him returning the kiss, and then her happily walking away, probably heading to her car.

"I knew once high school was done, you would be going to college and no doubt move on from her. I didn't want to tell you, cause I didn't want you to be down. Your dad was sick. You needed someone more than me. I told her once your dad gets better to leave you alone. That I would expose her. But you know Jade…"

"She probably manipulated you out of it. Like she'd done with me and this relationship. I know you had my back. I know this is the reason you didn't tell me. I'm not mad. Part of me wishes you hadn't kept it a secret, and there's this part which knows if the roles had been reversed, I most likely would have done the same."

I knew Jade was trouble, and maybe that was part of the reason I was excited to be with her. At the time it was exciting, but now that we were older. I could see her for what she truly was and I had a feeling if I told the guys about what happened with Reese they would be happy for me.

I didn't know how Jade was going to take the news once I broke up with her, and I really didn't care.

CHAPTER EIGHT

Reese

This was weird, everything was done that was supposed to happen. I'd spent the last four weeks tutoring the boys. They were all on their way to pass the year, and next week was the dance.

"What do you think about this, giving it a little color instead of starting again?" Aaliyah asked as she took out my long black dress. The last time I had any girl come over, was when I was around eleven and it was Jade. Aaliyah had been coming over the last few days, especially when I wasn't with the guys, and hey it was nice having some girl company. I'd been so busy with tutoring, college acceptance letters, etc., I had forgotten about the simple things. The type of things I used to crave when everyone made me feel like crap and how it was to be a girl. A girl with maybe a friend or two.

"You don't look enthusiastic for someone who has not only one guy taking you, but three of the hottest guys in school, one of which just so happens to be my twin."

I turned away from her and headed to my bed. I didn't know how to express myself sometimes because for such a long time, I never spoke to anyone. I'd been living in a shell, crying for someone to find me and now, well now it was something I dreamed about and at times didn't know how to handle it.

She sat next to me and faced me. "You know I feel like crap for not wanting to know you earlier. I was too busy listening to the shit that came out of Jade's mouth instead of trying to get to know you and I apologize."

I shook my head, "Don't sweat it."

"No. You shouldn't dismiss it. When some-one's done you wrong, and they're apologizing, then accept it. Let them know how they made you feel."

She rose her arm, and turned her hand into a

fist, then smiled as she said, "Stay strong. Be true to yourself. That's the only way you're going to win respect from anyone."

"By making them feel the way they made me feel?"

She shook her head. "By saying the truth dummy. You were made to feel like crap and you shouldn't have let that happen. I don't want you to feel that way again."

I bit on my lower lip.

"What if Jade comes back to the school, and ruins the dance?"

"Well, Alan said they took care of it. So I wouldn't worry about it. Besides, the only thing you have to worry about is how to look beautiful for the dance."

"The final year. The final dance."

"I can't fucking wait to get out of this place!" Aaliyah screeched.

She meant high school, I used to think like that. I couldn't wait. The place I once loved to hate, I didn't want to leave now, because I had a friend who I could count on and made me feel as if there wasn't anything in the world I couldn't do.

This was how she made me feel that day in the cafeteria, when I had my first lunch there. Something I never confessed to her before, and we would never have enough time together, because in a few short months we would be out of high school.

She couldn't wait. Whereas I wanted to savor every single second of it, until it ended.

CHAPTER NINE

J eff

I t was as if we had bonded in so many ways as we prepared for what started out as a dare, and ended with it feeling like it had been an honor. The idea of taking Reese Smith to the dance was probably one of the best things to happen in high school for me.

Our math scores were something we set out to achieve, but the time we spent getting to know it, felt all relative.

"Wow, you wouldn't think that you were going

to the dance, but just the mall!" Dad said as he cut his eye at me. I ignored him as he placed the red rose in my top pocket. I was ready to meet the guys at Howard's house. Before, his comments would wind me up, belittle me. Now, I didn't give a shit. Soon, I would be at university, and I wouldn't have to listen to this type of shit anymore. There was only one issue, and that was going to university meant that the bond and relationship I had with the guys could be a thing of the past.

I just needed my keys. Even if I did plan to be back tomorrow, I would stay in the suite for as long as possible.

*R*eady? Howard

*H*e sent a message letting me know that it was time. I had to be on my way. I didn't need a reminder. We said we would arrive at his house at six on the dot, and it wasn't even half past five. He was already checking up on me.

I slammed the door shut and headed to my jeep. I had a dirty grin on my face, one that the whole world would see at the dance, once we walked in with Reese.

A girl that I used to love to hate, now I couldn't think of anything better but just loving her. Even if it did mean sharing her.

~

"We're doing this, right?" I asked as we sat in the helicopter. So we went a little OTT. Everyone was going with limos and all that crap, however we wanted to go there with a bang. When the helicopter settled on the rooftop, we watched and heard the crowd cheer for us.

"This is nuts!" Reese screamed as she took off her headphones and passed them to the pilot.

"Only the best for our girl!" I shouted as I stepped up to the helicopter and took her hand. She looked absolutely stunning in her gold, flowing, silk dress, which was strapless. Her hair was pinned up exposing her neckline, and she had splatters of gold glitter in her hair and over her face. Reese was a natural beauty, and didn't need tons of makeup to stand out in a crowd. Not in my eyes.

"Damn, I need to get me three boyfriends, cause if this is what it feels like then me want some!" Aaliyah shouted out as Alan helped her out of the helicopter, too. He crossed his brow as if he wasn't comfortable with the idea of his sister being in a harem, but said nothing about it.

At the end of the day, he was in one, and couldn't make it out to be a bad thing, when he knew that it was far from that.

"You both look beautiful," Howard beamed as he stood at the other side of Reese and acknowledged that not only did Reese look spectacular but Aaliyah did too. She was in silver, and had exactly the same hairstyle as Reese. They took the helicopter together and now it was for us to lead them to the dance. Some part of me was nervous about Jade turning up and ruining it all. She'd left high school without completing her final year. We're not sure why, but Howard said that it was a blessing rather than a curse, her not being around today so we took it like that. One of life's mysteries that I didn't want to know why it'd happened, just happy that it had occurred.

"Wait. Time for a photo!" Howard's mom smiled as she proudly looked at her son.

"You okay?" I asked Reese, thinking that she was a little too quiet.

She nodded, while trying to hold back the tears. I took out my pocket square and gave it to her, so it wouldn't smudge her makeup.

"I know I dared you to take me, but all this. I mean, it's so much."

I winked at her. "It's only just begun. Now enjoy it."

She nodded her head, and stopped anymore tears from falling, as we started to take some poses, the typical ones taken at dances but not with three guys belonging to one girl. Howard's mom wasn't for it at first, but then she said being a Christian meant she shouldn't judge others, so as long as we were happy, she was happy too.

We cheered and laughed as we held on to Reese and pretended to drop her. She cried out at first, but when she realized that we were joking she laughed along.

We proceeded down the stairs to the dance. The dull, boring hall had been turned into a magical event with cupid and his flying arrows and hearts skillfully placed in parts in the hall.

There were heart cakes, cookies, and cups with hearts around it. There was no denying that Heather Jones', whose dream job was as a designer, and who was the senior in charge of the decorations, did a fantastic job.

"Look guys, there's even the Eiffel Tower over there."

Of course, the city of love, and the place that we promised we would take Reese to once we finished the year and had the time during the summer. Our tickets were booked, and our plan was to enjoy the evening.

We wouldn't pressure her, but take turns to dance and see how she wanted to roll with the night.

"The night's yours, my lady," Howard purred as he spun her around, and headed to the dance floor.

I grabbed Aaliyah's hand. "You want to show a white man how to dance!"

She giggled, "Please, you dance better than me."

Yeah, she had a point. I did spend a little too much time on TT. I mean that shit is fucking addictive once you get started, and Aaliyah had liked and commented one too many times on my videos. Music was my escape from reality. Baseball was, too, but at times I felt as if I needed to feel I was good at something more than the sport, especially when I'd spent most of my childhood listening to my dad tell me that I was a disappointment.

The night was early, but it was coming to an end far too quickly. Especially when they called out the King and Queen of the night. We may have had too much of a hand making sure that Reese was Queen. We'd made a pact that we didn't care which one of us were the King. I'd never been in a harem before, but I was learning about what it meant to make sure that there was no jealousy. We were all as important to her, as she was to us. It was the start of a beautiful relationship, one that I knew college wouldn't bring to a dramatic end.

"And the Queen tonight is Reese Smith. Come here and get your crown," Principal Williams called out. We cheered and roared, as she took to the stage, the tears she didn't want to fall out, couldn't be helped as she got all emotional and stepped up to the stage.

"Life is about changes, about taking risks and not only being in the same spot all the time. I did that when I started tutoring my three men, Jeff, Alan and Howard. It wasn't an easy ride, but they showed me that just because someone appears to be all tough on the outside, doesn't mean that they are like that on the inside. I blamed my one best friend that I had in middle school for making my life a misery. I never tried to make it better. Because it's easy to blame someone than to take responsibility for your own life. Soon, we'll be ending our journey at high school and embarking on adulthood. Put the childish paths behind you, and do better as you grow."

There was silence as she spoke. She said it

with such confidence as she wore the crown and addressed everyone. I think some, including Principal Williams, was shocked about the change in her confidence. I couldn't be prouder as I jumped in the air, clapped and applauded her for her speech.

It was short, but it said so many things in that short time. She'd grown, and I had too, from a jerk to a better person and I wanted to keep on feeling the way I did now.

"Now, it's time find out who will be Reese's King!"

Alan, Howard and I nodded, knowing it could be any one of us. Then as all three of our names were called out, we stood in shock.

"Well, the Queen does have three men, so it makes sense for Howard, Alan, and Jeff to be her Kings."

Shit, this really rocked us, as we patted each other on the back, and took to the stage. There weren't three crowns. We didn't need them, we had the most important person in our lives from here on out. It wasn't a phase, or a stage in our lives like high school.

The love we shared for Reese was for keeps. We kissed and hugged her, knowing that this was something we would talk about for years to come and cherish.

CHAPTER TEN

Reese

The dance was over, and we were in the Presidential suite of the Canyon Suites at the Phoenician, a Luxury Collection Resort in Scottsdale. I'd seen photos of it on the internet, and it looked as if it was worth every penny.

There was a living room with sofas facing the electric fire, and a wide-screen TV above it. The whole suite was neutrally decorated with spot-light lighting, but the part I loved the most was the wide-window doors facing the golf course. It was a mini-apartment in a hotel, and I loved the idea that we could get down and dirty together. And, I didn't have to worry about anyone complaining about my screams.

Jeff had booked us to have a special weekend together. This would be the first time that we were not just one-to-one, but instead I would be with all three of them. I was excited and frightened at the same time about the idea of it. Three men at once.

When they first suggested it, I wanted to cry. I dared them to take me to the dance, and somehow in the midst of it all, I didn't need to. They wanted to be with me.

Mom's face when she saw all three of them was priceless. For the first time that I could remember as a teen, she kissed me on the head and said, "You go tigress! Enjoy your teen years."

Her reaction to it all shocked me.

Once we were in the room, no more were they acting like the gentlemen that they were at the dance — it was the complete opposite as both Jeff and Howard put their hands on the back of my bra.

"Slow down, boys. I haven't even taken in the suite, and you guys are already wanting to get down and dirty."

Their hands moved from where they were, to the side of my hips, and then they backed away.

"You have no idea what you do to us. You send us fucking wild," Howard growled as he moved in front of me.

I didn't know I had that kind of power over them. I wondered if they were tipsy from the dance and this was the reason they were acting this way.

"You've had too much to drink," I smiled, as I moved to the beige leather sofa in the corner of the room. I needed to sit down, making it known that they were not the only ones that probably had too much to drink. I did too.

Howard knelt down in-between my legs, and then he slowly lifted my dress and stroked my legs.

"Let's move her to the table, we all want a piece of her."

I laughed, "And I don't have a say in the matter?"

"So, you don't want us to move you?" Jeff growled, as Howard had already taken the lead, and was moving me to the marble table which sat at the other side of the room; the dining space, with six chairs for us to sit down and eat together, but the boys had no interest in eating anything but my pussy, and anything else they could suck on.

I had made sure that I bought a black, sexy

lace bra and knickers for tonight. Usually, I didn't care about my underwear, anything comfortable was good, but since I'd been with not just one, but all three of them, I paid attention to such things, I was waxing now on a regular basis, buying sexy underwear, even buying a teddy the other day. I thought things like that were only for skinny girls, not curvy ones like me, but I was wrong. I enjoyed not only buying it, but wearing it the other day for Alan.

Howard started to kiss me gently where his hands once were, and then I realized this was the first time the three of us were together. So, my eyes darted around the dimly lit room to see that Jeff was taking in his surroundings by pacing the room, whereas Alan was just watching Howard. He hovered over me, and used his hand to slip off one shoe and then the other as his intentions were to please me. I laid down into the sofa, taking in the magic of his kisses.

Alan was no longer watching, but tugging at the top of my dress, so I lifted up, making it easier for him to take it from the back. As he did that, he took off my off-the-shoulder bra, and then started to gently stroke my breasts.

Howard pulled down my dress, exposing my body and then he traced a finger around my stomach, while Alan was pleasuring me from the top onwards. I could tell that Howard's mission was from the waist below.

Howard lifted up my legs and rested them gently while bending them on the table.

"I want to taste you so badly, feel your cum on the tip of my tongue."

My black thong became a thing of the past as his tongue moved from tasting my pussy lips to sucking and licking his way inside.

The more I moaned, the deeper he went in-between my legs, until they started to flop to the side as I became weak.

Alan was shifting and massaging my breasts. My rock hard nipples were gently being bitten by him. I was completely at his mercy.

"You taste so fucking good," Howard said as he opened my legs wider. This was when I completely lost control and started to scream.

"Yes, don't stop!" I was so close to coming, but I was trying to hold back for as long as I could, because I didn't want it to end.

"My cock feels like a loaded gun. I'm ready..." I heard Jeff growl, before I had a chance to recover from coming on Howard's tongue.

I stroked his dick as I saw it in full view.

"You're such a big boy."

He chuckled, "And a dirty one!" As Howard handed him a towel, he wiped in between my legs, and began to rub his balls against the entrance of my pussy. Alan started to make animal noises, and I knew what he needed, he needed release. So, I started to undo his pants and expose his cock. I put it in my hand then started to work it. The head of his cock was against my lips, as I started to lick around it.

Jeff stuck his cock into my dripping pussy and then I couldn't even scream, as he showed no mercy thrusting in and out of me. I was so fucking wet. He used one hand to hold on to my leg, then placed it over his shoulder. I couldn't see as I started to focus on giving Alan what he so desperately wanted and that was to come.

Jeff just kept pumping me deeper, and my breasts bounced as Alan thrusted deeper inside of me. It was as if Jeff got a kick out of it, as he pulled back, the moment of surprise. The one thing that I did love about being with Jeff, he was always creative whenever we had sex. He put his cock against the tip of my pussy lips, giving me the chance to focus on the head that I was giving Alan. I took him in deeper, using my fingers to tease his balls, and his cock to go deeper into my throat.

It was as if I knew how to make him cum. As he roared like a fucking lion and his cum shot into my mouth, I let go of his limp cock, and then

I knew Jeff would only give me a second to recover as Alan rolled off the side of the sofa on to the floor.

"Fuck!" Was the last word I heard as Jeff took complete control.

"Argh!" I screamed out. The louder I yelled, the more he was fucking me, taking me over the edge. I started to shake and I felt as if I saw darkness as his cum shot inside of me. His own legs shook as he dropped my leg, and then like Alan, he rolled to the floor.

"I didn't think that I had any energy left in me," I whispered as I tried to get up, but all the intensity of the events which had taken place had sucked every last piece of energy out of me.

"Here, here," Howard said as he lifted me in his arms and then carried me to what looked like a King-sized bed. The neutrally decorated room had a candle chandelier in the middle, and a sofa next to it. I wondered if all three of us could fit on the King-size bed, but I was too tired to think about that. All I wanted to do was sleep, as the curtains hadn't been closed and it was dark. He laid me on the bed, while being careful not to trip on the center table near the sofa.

"We've exhausted you," he said as he delicately put my body on the bed. I wanted to know what the guys would do, but I was too tired to ask.

"Rest, we'll be here when you wake up."

I protested, "But, we're supposed to be together all night long."

He kissed me on the forehead, then my cheeks and finally my lips.

"Reese Smith, I dare you to sleep, so that we can do this all over again. Don't worry about us. We'll be here waiting for you. Not only tonight, but every night."

I could see sincerity written all over his face. I closed my eyes, and heard gentle footsteps leave the room. I didn't know what the three guys were going to do, but I believed Howard's words. They would be waiting for me, and I would reward them, deeply.

*R*eese

*T*hey say that everything happens for a reason, maybe Jade's bullying, as crap as it had been at the time, had to happen so that I would be where I am now.

"Girl, you really went out with this beauty treatment," Aaliyah chuckled as our masseuses had left the gym where they'd set up the tables for us to have our massages.

"Yeah, you know me. I don't do anything small. Always big."

She chuckled, "Like have two sets of twins. I

know. I get it. You don't have to tell me. You've really got the life."

There was a sound of sadness in her voice. We'd kept in touch since she left for college, but I'd only been able to visit once. With a household of babies, I didn't get the chance to travel as much as I wanted, not that I was complaining, being a mom was more than I could ever dream it was and more.

"Do your parents visit?"

I shrugged, "No. They say that I'm an embarrassment living with three men, even if they are on the road sometimes. The only time I even have them around is off-season and during the holidays, at times."

She laughed as she slapped her hand on the table.

"That's a good thing. It gives down there a rest!" She said, pointing to my vagina, which was true, I couldn't deny that. At times trying to satisfy the three of them was a little much.

"You know since the birth of Ben and Dwight.." my first set of twins, which was a surprise to me, and the reason why I never went to college, "they've been doting dads, and it's been more about comforting, and snuggles on the sofa than it has been about sex."

. . .

*S*he smiled, "That must be nice though. Having them at your beck and call."

I shook my head. "No, it's nothing like that. It's more about the mutual respect we have for each other. It goes a long way. Like clearly Ben and Dwight are Alan's kids. As for Sharon and Claire…"

"Jeff's! No doubt with their piercing green eyes. It says it all. The part that makes me laugh the most is the fact they call them Dad, Daddy and Pa. Who came up with that idea?"

I jumped off the bench, as I proudly nodded my head.

"I did. There's stupid little things that we didn't think of at first, but it all works. I thought I would be huge, especially the first time around, but breastfeeding helped me to lose loads of weight."

She joined me as I started to head out of the gym to the garden, where the ladies were preparing our spas to do our pedicures and manicures.

"But you know that they loved you the way you were. You make me look bad. It's as if I've had four kids, not you."

"You look smoking hot. Don't let anyone tell you otherwise."

We both laughed at the thought of me using her words to make her feel better. We had a connection, one which I'd found not only with Aaliyah but with a couple of mom's in the paternal group that I'd joined. Some moms were jealous at first. Not only did I have one hottie as a partner, but three. I didn't think of them that way, even if they were all sexy as hell in different ways.

"So, no man for you still?" I asked out of curiosity, hoping she would tell me a little more about her love life before the guys showed up with the kids.

"Nope. I miss Arizona. NY is cool, but sometimes you feel a little lost. In Phoenix at least, I would bump into the odd person. Now, I just don't know anyone."

I choked, thinking that she couldn't be saying what I think she was trying to say.

"You're trying to say that the stylish and most popular girl in high school is no more that girl."

As we reached the garden, and we spotted the spas and the guys heading our way with the kids in tow, I knew our conversation was going to come to an end.

"You hear about Jade and the court case?"

I did indeed, even if I tried to stay out of it.

"Yep, her ex got a divorce and three years in

prison. What I didn't get was what happened to her?"

She laughed, "What should you care? She disappeared, I think out of embarrassment. Her family moved to LA and there was even a rumor of her being pregnant."

Now the pennies dropped, before we could even finish our little gossip session about why she left so suddenly at the end of the year. She had a baby. It made sense now that she said it.

"Ah, so what are you both gossiping about?" Alan asked as he greeted both Aaliyah and I with kisses on our cheeks. Our sons, both Trouble 1 and 2 as Alan liked to call them, started tugging on both sides of my robe. So much for our relaxing spa day, it was clearly going to come to an end.

"Leave Ma and Auntie alone," Jeff said as he scooped them in his arms. He blew kisses in the air and as quick as he was in our presence, he was out of it again.

Howard left the stroller to the side, and then came to plant a big kiss on my lips and hug me.

"The twins are sleeping. I'm going to put them up and get a nap myself. I hope that you're enjoying your day so far."

I nodded my head, and kissed him again. I missed him the most, because he seemed to be going through so much, if it wasn't one thing, then it was another and he could never travel back home as much at the other guys. We texted, did video calls, but it was never the same.

"Boys if you would excuse us, we're going to keep enjoying our spa day, and you guys can do baby duty. Agreed?"

Aaliyah clarified, as I kissed Howard again, and remembered the feeling of being in his arms as I took in his musk scent. I closed my eyes and broke our hug.

Alan slapped my butt cheekily then he helped Howard with the stroller. I watched them with a grin of joy. Tonight, Howard would be rewarded with my affection and love, the other two would have to wait. Aaliyah was right, it was nice having three men at your beck and call. They were home, which was my house, and they always obeyed my rules.

Sarwah Creed is the author of The FlirtChat series. When she's not writing, then she's running, reading and listening to music. She lives with her three children in Madrid.

Learn more about Sarwah by connecting with her on social media:

Newsletter ---- http://eepurl.com/g0cLoH

I had three hot SEALs with sexy eyes and bodies, and they all wanted the same thing.

Me.

My ex, Rick, dumped me. He didn't know I was pregnant at the time, and I hated him with a passion for it. Yet, the mistakes of my past had led me back to him. He'd moved on with another, who was nice, but the painful memories of the past kept taunting me.

A planned wedding.

A device to help me stay in the country.

Three ex-SEALs wanted me to get married for different reasons. Andre had a custody battle. He was a family man and promised to help me win my children back. Back home with me, where they belonged.

Cole was the one with the looks. Ladies fell at his feet. We spoke the same language and it was nice to speak to someone who understood me in my native language.

Brad was lonely, he wanted someone to love.

The struggle to decide which one of the three should be my future husband became harder every day because I'd been dumped and rejected before. I hated the idea of it happening again.

I had to trust my heart.

It was so hard when, until now, I'd struggled to trust anyone.

How could I trust all three?

Maite

The day had finally arrived. I had to be brave and face the music. I knew I was meeting my custody lawyer, the one which charged me by the hour. I had to get there on time for the meeting with my ex, Rick. My heart was beating out of control as I adjusted my black pencil skirt and blazer. They were too tight. I didn't possess a suit of my own, but luckily, Lara, my best friend, was willing to lend me one. If things did go to court, then most likely I would have to wear it every day. Then again, if it went to court, I would need to sell a kidney to pay for my lawyer.

I ran up to the door, thinking about my babies, imagining a glow in their eyes every day and knowing I had to be a part of their lives. I'd left them once; I couldn't do it again. I knew they were well looked after and had money, a lot more than I had to offer them. The one thing I had which was priceless, was *love*.

"Ms. Maite Rodriguez to see Harvard Pickles," I said to the receptionist.

"Mate. They're expecting you," the petite blond receptionist said as her eyes lit up.

I corrected her, "My name is Maite, you pronounce it Mytea."

She ignored me as she stood and told her colleagues to cover her.

I watched her, frozen and unable to move, as she moved to the side. She pointed to one of the entrance doors, then pressed a button and it opened.

"Come here, and we'll head up." She smiled as I walked toward her at the back of the receptionist's desk. I felt so intimidated standing next to her. She towered over me with her tall, slender figure. I'd never worried about my size. I was an average height, with an hour-glass figure, but here in the lawyer's office, with women who most likely ate what I had for breakfast in pieces which would last them all week long, I felt out of place.

From my cheap perfume to my high-heels, which only made me a couple of inches taller, I felt...less than. She wore stilettos, and as she smiled at me, the same smile she seemed to give everyone that passed her by, I wondered what she thought of me. Back home, in Mexico, I wouldn't care. I didn't give a shit what anyone thought of me, but there was something about being in L.A. that brought about this type of insecurity. Lara, my best friend and savior in this big mess, said this was the issue with being a foreigner: you felt as if everyone was looking and laughing at you, when deep down, there was nothing of the sort going on. It was all in our heads.

"Right, follow me, and I'll lead the way." She didn't wait for me to reply, and I followed her like a lamb being led to the slaughter. I'd lost my kids once, there was no option to do it again. If I did, my heart would sink and I would die of natural causes.

"Everyone makes mistakes, *cariño*. Doesn't mean they have to spend the rest of their lives suffering for them."

Lara's words were ringing through my ears as we approached the elevator. The pretty blonde receptionist smiled, but this time, I was too nervous to return it. I couldn't be bothered with fake pretenses, not right now.

I looked down at the floor. I couldn't see my reflection in the pale tiles, but I knew if I could, I would see the tears which were about to fall.

"In we go!" she commanded, and I could tell she was going to say something to break the ice, but I felt defeated as she stuck her arm out and pressed the button to what seemed to be the top floor.

Mierda!

My vertigo was sure to kick in. As if I wasn't nervous enough as it was.

"We'll be there soon. This is the private elevator."

I stuttered, "It's so high up."

Her face changed from being stone-cold to warm, as if she could see the fear in my eyes and she no longer gave me the fake smile she offered everyone as she wrapped her arm around me and whispered, "Don't think of going up, just straight."

I looked up at her, the tears which I held back for so long flowing freely. I didn't care if I cried in front of her. It seemed silly to worry about such things in that moment.

"I used to suffer, too. It helps. Just close your eyes and think about it."

I did as she said and took a deep breath. She was right. The higher we went, the more I felt as if we were going forward, not upward.

I giggled like a child as the doors chimed and I opened my eyes. "It worked!"

She held my hand, her fingers long and slender, but warm. Whereas mine were just sweaty from being high up. I avoided looking at the floor number, because I knew if I saw which floor we were on I would panic again.

As I stepped out, Rick was standing, smiling, with his arms crossed. Every reason I'd fallen in love with him was staring at me. I was trying to hate his big grin, emerald eyes, and dark hair—everything about him, really. He was someone else's, not mine. I couldn't think of him in that way, even if I wanted to.

"Well. Seems everything is all done."

He brushed past me, heading for the elevator. The same one I'd just stepped out of, with the help of the receptionist. I spun around, but it was too late. The doors were closing, and I was left breathless. I spotted my lawyer, who'd been hired to help me with my custody battle through the glass door opposite the elevator.

"Oh good, you made it!" Her dark eyes spun around to me. She was Lara's lawyer, as well, which was how I found her. Lara said that she helped win an impossible case, but she didn't offer any more information than that. I didn't know if it was her case or someone else's.

She was in her forties, so I knew she had experience. She had dark hair, like myself, which she constantly wore in a bun. Like the receptionist, she was near to a size zero and she always seemed to be in a hurry, as if she was anxious. I'd seen her one time smoking in the parking lot and figured that was probably why she was always in a hurry, to get outside and smoke.

"You told me twelve," I said, hating her attitude. She gave me the impression that she didn't like me; she was always so cold to me. Lara said that she is my lawyer, not my friend. Yet, I still would like the person representing me to act like I'm their client, not some hobo on the street bothering them for money.

She nodded. "Yes, and you should have been earlier than the said time. If it was important enough for you to be part of the meeting, then you would have done it. I expected you to be the first one at the door," she scolded, her dark eyes cut at me. The way she looked at me, I wondered if it was a good idea for her to represent me, because she should have told me to get here earlier, but she didn't. She wasn't looking after my best interest and felt comfortable embarrassing me in front of others. I felt my face turn red, not only because they'd already had the meeting, but the way she spoke to me too. As if I was completely stupid.

"Sorry, I should have told you that they were all here. They'd been here for a while," the receptionist muttered next to me.

A foreigner. Once again, this was how I was being treated. There were rules which I should have automatically known, and I didn't.

"So, what now?" I shrugged, not having the strength to argue as I laid my purse on the table. Lara said I should carry it. It made me seem important, even if all it contained were her house keys and my phone.

"We'll talk after the wedding," my lawyer said, as she shot up and adjusted her red suit. She moved the chair she was sitting on away from her, as if it annoyed her the same way my late appearance had done.

"Wedding?"

"Lara did say you were slow, but I didn't expect you to be this slow…"

Once again, she cut her eyes at me. If she was anyone else, if I didn't need her so badly, then I would tell her to stick it where the sun doesn't shine. But Lara said she was good. Real good. And I needed her, not only for her expertise, but because she was free for this first meeting with Rick, a favor for Lara, but after that I would have to pay if we needed to go to court. This part she made clear, she said that hopefully, it wouldn't come to that.

I realized that she wanted this meeting to go according to plan, most likely without me being here, so everything would be settled. Previously, she'd asked if I could pay to go to court. I reassured her. She scanned me from head to waistline, because I was growing red with the lie. I was crap at lying, no matter how hard I tried, and she could see straight through me.

"Your wedding. You know, the one to the SEAL. I can't remember his name. It doesn't matter," she waved, as if there was a mosquito buzzing around her and she needed to get rid of it. I saw nothing. The more she spoke, the more I realized she wasn't trying to get rid of an imaginary mosquito, but just me.

"When you've done that, then we can agree on some schedule. Until then, four weeks and two days from now, you'll hear from me."

I felt as if she was speaking another language. I didn't understand a word that had come out of her mouth.

Wedding?

Who said anything about a wedding?

"You look as if you need something stronger than coffee. Wait here, I'll get you something," the receptionist said.

She had no idea, because I didn't want to seem like more of a fool than my lawyer had made me feel when she said that I turned up late. None of this made any sense. The purpose of the meeting was to talk about my rights to see my children. Not a wedding. I did need something stronger, because apparently, I was about to get married.

But there was just one problem.

I didn't have a boyfriend.

Let alone a fiancé.

I sat in what appeared to be a board room. Well, that is what the sign on the door said as we entered. In had my drink in hand, then I heard my phone chime. I was about to look at it, but then the receptionist came to my side.

"Take as long as you like, just leave the drink and the elevator will take you to the ground floor. *Buena suerte,* Maite."

Then she kissed me on the cheek, I was taken aback by her kindness. I'd done nothing to deserve it, but I needed it more than she'd ever know. I hadn't slept all night because I was nervous about the meeting. I'd spent more time getting ready and preparing myself mentally for being here today than I should have, and in the space of a few seconds I'd been made to feel so insignificant and as if my one wish, to be with my babies, was something I'd given up the right to as soon as I'd left them in Rick's building.

I made a note to find out her name and somehow pay her back for her kindness. There was only one thing I did well, one skill I was proud of, and that was cooking. I would make her a *Tinga de Pollo* once I got back home and bring it to her the next day. I didn't have much money, but I knew how to cook. It was something personal, so I hoped she would appreciate it more than if I'd bought her a donut or something.

My eyes darted to my phone where I noticed a message from Rick.

Meet me in Starbucks, 555 W 5th St in twenty. Rick

I used to hate his impersonal messages, they always felt as if they were commanding me to do something. No questions asked: Rick calls, and you go running. I hated his attitude at times. That's the crazy thing about being in love. Sometimes I would think of it as being so sexy, I would be like, *Oh, how I love how he takes charge!* Now the very thing I had deemed as sexy was just plain rude. We weren't together anymore, so I didn't have to accept it.

Yet, as much as I was telling myself that, realistically I was kidding myself. I had to be on his good side. He had my kids.

I quickly checked to see if I could make it there in twenty minutes. I could be there in fifteen minutes if I took a taxi and half-an-hour if I walked. Well, I didn't have the money or luxury of taking a taxi, so he would have to wait.

The almighty Rick Steele could wait for a while. I'd done the same thing when he walked out of the door and left me, like a scared mouse. He ran away without having the decency to say goodbye. The woman whose heart he'd broken had to remain in this building and not let him know that after all this time I was still hurting after the way he treated me. He didn't deserve to know that even after all he did, seeing him right now made me weak at the knees. No. I would do the same to him as he'd done to me. I'll make him wait and suffer, not knowing if I was going to turn up, or if he would ever see my face again. I would give him a taste of his own medicine.

All the hurt and pain of the past rushed through me and I decided I wouldn't just stay here for another twenty, but I would stretch it to thirty minutes. I kept dismissing it, thinking I could leave, I could face him. As soon as I stood up, I found the tears I'd held back so I needed to calm down and focus on the twins. I couldn't break down in front of him, I wouldn't give him the satisfaction of seeing me cry. He didn't deserve anything but pain from me. He was my only ticket to getting them back. My babies were the only thing worth living for, I had nothing else, and going back home to Mexico wasn't an option if I wanted to live. My Uncle would kill me in a heartbeat if I showed up back there.

I had to compose myself and make sure that I put everything in perspective. There was too much to lose by blowing Rick off and not showing my face. Something I couldn't afford to do, even if the stubborn part of me wanted nothing more.

~

My heart was beating rapidly and I was uncontrollably sweating. I'd decided to wait thirty minutes, but ended up staying a lot longer than that. I was kidding myself. This was all bullshit. I wasn't over Rick. We'd been together for three years. Then one day he just up and left with no explanation. He left some cash on the bedside table, and took his things from our one-bedroom apartment.

Now my ex and kids were living with his fiancée, Katie. Rick had moved on, and not only did he have kids with me, but her too.

Every cloud has a silver lining and that saying fell true when I was six months pregnant and I couldn't work as a stripper anymore, let alone have any other job in the club. Even being a cleaner wasn't an option at that point. A girl in the strip club I used to work in was obsessed with social media, so she was able to figure out where they lived. She claimed everyone who posted about their lives left a window for stalkers. They wanted all details to be known about them. I didn't know if it was to gloat or for others to know their every movement.

Rick was a triplet and considered himself to be the eldest. He had two brothers, Stan and Pete. I'd met them a few times, but I wouldn't say that all three of us were friends, exactly. They may have been triplets, but they were completely different personality wise.

Rick was the strict one out of the three. It was probably the reason why they looked up to him. Pete was the carefree one, the one Rick claimed would never settle down, and Stan was the nerd who spent way too much time on the computer. Rick prided himself on being the one that held them together, but behind closed doors he was a wounded SEAL. I turned a blind eye to his drinking and mood swings. When I was pregnant, I spent more time thinking about why he left, and the fact that as much as I painted this picture of us being so happy, realistically we weren't. We were two people together trying to get over their painful pasts.

After I found out I was pregnant and needed to find Rick, I discovered that Pete loved to post on social media nearly every single day. Sometimes two or three times a day. It was strange, because the little time we spent together, I never thought of him as that type of guy, but then I remembered the girl telling me that you don't really know someone until you've seen them on social media.

Pete gave me an opportunity to turn into a stalker, and it didn't take long to figure out where they lived, because I had nothing better to do.

I couldn't strip and I took on odd jobs because

I needed the money seeing as I was about to have an extra mouth to feed, or so I thought at the time. I never knew I was carrying twins. I had no idea how I was going to do it. I began to panic, because I knew the odd cleaning job wouldn't be an option and I had no idea how I was going to feed myself, let alone my baby.

I was growing bigger, with no medical insurance. I knew the only trip I would be making to the doctor was when I was ready to give birth.

The girls had got together to help with the Silver health insurance plan. It meant that the only thing I would be seeing a doc for was to give birth. I avoided any visit because I didn't want the cost to go up. I promised to pay them back, but they knew as well as I did that there was no way I was going to be able to do that. I didn't have the money, but they felt like crap knowing what Rick had done to me., even though it was never their fault. Once a guy was rough in one way or another, we all went out of our way to help each other. We knew girls like us didn't get much in life, we'd all come from rough backgrounds, so we made ourselves a family of misfits. It was rare that one of us was lucky and we got out of the lifestyle. I thought, for just a moment, that I was one of those girls. After he left and I could no longer work, I remembered his angry mood swings, the drinking binges we would go on together. There was nothing romantic or pretty about our relationship, but at the time it felt as if it was everything. As if someone really saw me, and wanted to be with me. When you have nothing and someone pays you some attention, it feels like everything. Rick did back then, and he knew it. That was the part that hurt the most.

I tried to put those feelings aside as I reached the Starbucks and saw him sitting and waiting for me.

Forty-five minutes late.

Some part of me hoped he would leave and I wouldn't have to face him. I'd sat in the board-room thinking I was ready to face him, but who was I kidding? There were too many mixed feel-ings to dismiss in a few years, let alone minutes.

"You're late," Rick said to the table, without facing me. The moment I walked in he turned his head away from me, his eyes on the table, as if he was more nervous than I.

"You're lucky I came. I so-o-o didn't want to, Rick. I so…" I stuttered trying to get the words out as all my emotions flushed out of me.

He put his hand on mine as he stood up, this

time removing his sunglasses and looking directly at me. I could have sunk into his arms as all the old feelings, the good ones, the ones I'd tried to keep under lock and key, came to the surface. I didn't know who I hated more, him or myself, for making me feel this way. I should hate him. No, I did hate him. I was getting confused, thinking I felt something for this man. No nothing. I had to remember how he abandoned me. It had to be in the forefront of my mind, otherwise I would regret coming, I would think of myself as weak and if I was weak then there was no way that I was going to get my kids back.

Never.

I should want to stay as far away from him as possible, but I couldn't and I had to remember that. I had to focus on only them. Nothing more. Definitely not him. He wasn't worth it.

"I know. I deserve to wait for an eternity, but we have to do this. Otherwise, I wouldn't have bothered sending you the message."

He said it so casually that it annoyed me, so I slapped him as hard as I could, but it probably just grazed his face. He was so big, whereas I was so small, and my hand hurt a lot more by giving him the slap than the pain I intended to inflict on him.

He rubbed his cheek to confirm what I'd

already suspected. The slap had done nothing
to him.

"I deserved that."

So I did it again, hoping this time to make an
impact on him. Just a little of the pain and fear of
having to go back home to Mexico I'd been
carrying around with me since he left.

Did it make me feel better? Not really, because
everyone was looking at us. I was waiting for him
to react to it, but he only looked at me, a tear
welling up in his eye. Seeing it brought back the
memories of us being together. The times he
would be crying in my arms as he talked about
the death of both his parents.

I sucked in a breath then slumped down. He
shifted to the side, out of my field of vision. I
didn't know where he was going, but he returned
a few minutes later, after I'd caught my breath
and tried to calm down, and he was holding a hot
chocolate with marshmallows on top. The same
gift he used to offer, which always made me
smile, as we talked about our painful pasts. This
time I would drink it, but I wouldn't smile. I
wanted to keep hitting him. I'd never slapped
anyone in my life, but I didn't hesitate to do it
one more time, before he sat.

"You left me. You didn't even say goodbye.
You were gone. Just like that." The words were

rushing out of my mouth like hot air as he pushed the hot chocolate closer to me.

Did he really think it would make me feel better? I would cry. Smile. Then, we would talk about the missing years? He simply nodded and his silence angered me even more.

"I was weak and a coward. I wasn't in a good place, but that's no excuse for how I treated you. A slap is nothing compared to what I deserved for my cowardice."

There were times where I'd sat and rehearsed the words I would say to him. One time, it resulted in me learning some killer moves, as if I was one of Charlie's Angels and I knew kung-fu. I would act like some ninja or something and I would kick him and punch him until he was black and blue, then I would walk away with a smile on my face, knowing the pain I'd inflicted on him was enough to bring my broken heart some semblance of satisfaction. The disappointment of knowing the slaps I'd given him were nothing in comparison to the way he made me feel back then, and even worse now, gnawed at me. He'd hurt me, broke my heart, a pain which I'd experienced once before when I was fifteen and my parents died.

I snatched my hand away from his. He had no fucking right to touch me.

"Don't touch me. If it wasn't for Kylie's obsession with social media and Pete posting about your club and your lifestyle, then I wouldn't have figured out where you lived. I didn't even know I was pregnant. You left and who knows what would have happened to the twins back then?"

"What do you mean?"

"Well, I was desperate. I didn't know I was pregnant when you left, and imagine the shock when I did find out that I was carrying not one baby, but two."

I paused for a second, trying to catch my breath. I shut my eyes and tried to explain to him exactly what had happened in the past.

"I didn't know what to do. This wasn't entirely true...I could have had a termination. The girls had them all the time. I was no stranger to witnessing them, but the difference was that I saw what they became when they had them. It was so ugly. Numb. Dead inside. Alcoholics, or even worse, they became hooked on drugs to ease the pain. Not knowing what day or even month we were in. Most of the time they didn't even care."

He said nothing. He didn't even look at me, but that didn't stop me from taking a sip of the hot chocolate and retelling the past.

"I waited for you, Rick. I fucking waited. I

thought maybe you would realize the mistake you'd made and come back to me. Even when I hit four months, I didn't give up. I kept waiting, living in some sick fantasy land, thinking that you would miss me, come back, and we would be one happy family. All you needed was time."

Our eyes locked as if he'd woken from the place he went to for a few seconds. I remembered how much I used to love looking into his green eyes and finding myself lost in them. I hated myself even more now for feeling that way. I should hate him. I wanted to hate him. No, I *needed* to, for my own sanity. He'd done me wrong, and belonged to another. Whenever I drifted into the good memories of the past, I needed to be brought back to reality by the fact that he left me.

"I thought about it. I won't deny that. I did for a long time, wonder about you. I knew that I needed to go back to find out if you were okay. It was the least I could do. I knew you were illegal and at any moment, you could get sent back. When I did have the guts to do it, I heard you left the club, a conversation in which I had with one of the girls who'd left the old club to join our new one. I just figured you'd moved on. She never said you were pregnant, and in all honesty I didn't ask any questions. I was a fucking pussy, not asking for details to make myself feel better. I knew that if you weren't all right then I was responsible for it. A responsibility that I wasn't willing to own."

He shocked me, because I never knew or even thought that he would bother to think of me from the moment he left.

"You checked up on me?"

He nodded, not saying anything more as I replayed his words in my mind. He said he asked casually about me, that wasn't the same thing as checking up on me.

I sipped on my chocolate, while he continued to stare at the table. I didn't know what to say to him. I felt as if I'd said enough, and if he apologized a thousand times, it wouldn't make up for what he did.

"I thought you did it to punish me," he practically whispered.

"What?"

I didn't understand what he meant by that. What did I do in all this that was so wrong?

"I assumed you had some man in Mexico, or even here. So you had the kids and decided to dump them on me as some form of punishment for leaving. But it didn't take long for me to figure out you hadn't left them because you were riding into the sunset with someone, you'd left them because you were in trouble. I should have done something, anything, but I somehow decided the best thing I could do to help you was to look after our kids."

I hated the idea of him knowing me so well, but there was no denying we had a past filled not only with the painful memory of him leaving, but the good times too.

"Yeah, immigration just seemed to be everywhere and I thought it was a matter of time before they caught up with me. I was lucky that the girls pitched in to help pay for their delivery. Otherwise, who knows what would have happened?"

He punched his legs, and I looked up, startled, and noticed a tear had swelled up in his eye. Rick wasn't a man for showing any emotion, especially in public. Maybe this really was a different Rick and the one who'd left me behind was under lock and key.

"Fuck! I'm so sorry, please forgive me…"

He pleaded as he went on bended knees next to me. I couldn't even look at him as he took my hands and continued to plead with me. The idea of him being on his knees and everyone watching should have given me pleasure, as he appeared to feel like shit about the past. He should.

"I only found out they were twins when I went into premature labor. I'd never had a hospital visit or check-up. All I knew was that the price would be more to have them, but I had no choice."

I started to cry, unable to fight the tears any longer_as I started talking about the time I decided to leave my babies. The hardest decision of my life.

"I knew where you lived. I even followed Pete home once when I was six months pregnant. I thought about telling him then. I toyed with what to do every single day. Then, they came early. As soon as I left the hospital, I knew I couldn't stay with Lara. Not indefinitely. I had no income. Nothing.

It felt stupid to even think about adoption, especially when I knew where you lived."

There are so many options out there, but they're all restricted to people who are legal residents of the country. I didn't want my kids being brought up in a system where they would be known as the kids dumped at the hospital or in trash cans. Girls I'd worked with had done that, I saw their misery at the idea of having such a painful decision to make. They would go for backstreet abortions, which lead to some of them being unable to work again, or they would have the baby and as a result of their decisions, the baby would be deformed. They had to live with the painful decision they had made. Most of them couldn't cope with a baby, let alone one with special needs.

I could go on to tell him all the things that happened and what was going through my mind in detail, but we weren't friends. He'd hurt me, led me to desperation.

"Every day was painful. Lara said she thought I was suffering from Postpartum Depression. Everything that should happen naturally as a new mother didn't happen for me. It was as if I was missing the maternal instinct. I felt like a failure, because I couldn't produce milk and I didn't go out anymore. We lived in a one-bedroom apartment with her daughter, and I was on her sofa with not one child, but two. Of course I was fucking depressed. The mere thought of going out would send me into a panic attack thinking that immigration would see me and take me away from those babies and sign my death warrant by sending me back over the border. I was living in a fucking nightmare. You wanted to know the past? Let's talk," I said coldly as I took back my hands.

He wiped at the tears now falling from his eyes and regained composure in his chair.

We said nothing. I sipped on my chocolate and he didn't move an inch. Anger and hurt was too fresh in my mind. I couldn't sit and have small talk with him. I had to leave. I was just about to stand up and do so, the remains of my hot chocolate still burning in my throat, but then he spoke.

"Lara," he chuckled lightly. "Wow, how's she doing? And the little one?"

"Fine."

This wasn't a fucking reunion and I wasn't about to start sharing stories with him. I shouldn't have come, this was a mistake. A big fucking mistake. Like the time I fell in love with Rick Steele.

"I know you hate me. And I don't blame you. But I think we can make this work for us all. I've really been trying with the twins. To raise them, and do right not only by them, but by you too."

Mierda!

Was he expecting me to get down on my knees and praise him?

"This was a mistake!" I shot up.

He was trying to be nice, but seeing him again after over two years… I thought I would have calmed down. Then again, I was doing a lot better than before. I couldn't imagine seeing and speaking to him like this if I'd had the balls to confront him back when I found out where they'd lived.

"I just want to make things right. I can't undo the past, but I can make the future better. I know some guys and well, my wedding's in less than a few days time. And Pete just renovated a house, which he's looking to sell. We were thinking of introducing the guys to you and then…well, we'll see how it goes."

He stood up next to me, his words were coming out so fast, and we both knew that if he didn't explain himself soon, I would be gone. Because he couldn't have just said what I'd thought he'd said.

"You want to pimp me out to your friends and in return, you'll let me see my kids?"

He leaned forward and spoke quietly, while motioning for me to sit down.

"Not like that. You're illegal, and this way—if you get married—it could be a good way for you to stay here and be part of their lives."

I sat down, thinking my English is really going bad, because I just don't understand a word coming out of his mouth.

"We?"

"Yes, Katie and I."

His wife-to-be. I wasn't ready for jealousy to creep into my mind, and he must have seen it, too, because he took my hand.

I shoved him away and spat, "Well thank you

and your new wife-to-be for your generous offer, but I was a stripper, not a prostitute, so I'll kindly decline."

It was a stupid thing to say, because we both knew when a client paid top dollar for a private show, it didn't mean I was just stripping, I used to do a lot more than that before we got together. He jumped up, shaking his head in a panic.

"No. You have it all wrong. I don't mean like that. Of course, I don't think of you like that. Look!" Once again, he was touching me, so I snatched my shoulder away from him, stopping only once I'd reached the door, ready to leave him.

"Come to the wedding. Meet the guys. Move into the house whenever you want. Then we can see how things go. If it doesn't work out, we'll come up with another solution. I mean, I want the kids to know who you are. You're their mom and you hold a special place in their hearts."

His eyes were pleading with me, just as they had done so many times in the past. I shoved past him to open the door. I didn't reply, I just ran in the direction I had come from. It didn't matter if I was running to Lara's or not, I just knew I had to get as far away from him as possible. Once I was far enough, I looked at my phone, it'd been beeping like crazy as I ran.

. . .

The address is 8676 Melvin Ave, Northridge. As I said, stay at the house. Come to the wedding. The invitation is at the house. See how it goes. I want you to be part of our kids lives.

I was just about to shove the phone in my pocket, but I decided to reply to him anyway.

It hurts too much Rick. You keep saying our kids' lives. But not me.

I had to tell him the truth. I would be lying to him and myself if I didn't admit that knowing he wasn't part of the equation was the part that was hurting the most.

I'd moved on.

I really had.

Until, I saw him once again and all those feelings of the past came flooding back in.

He wasn't mine.

I had to flush them out. I couldn't break down

again, because if I did, not only would I lose myself again, but my kids too. This time not for a while, but for good.

Free with Kindleunlimited. Click here to get your copy!